MOPPARELLA

ILLUSTRATED BY BAKTHI ROSS

(Pictures are illustrated with an optical mouse)

Author Bakthi Ross © 2014
ABN 19943908

For information or to order additional books, please write to
malaross27@yahoo.com.au
OR PHONE 07-54987214
Or order on createspace.com.

ISBN   978 192 222 0097

192 2220094

Once in a hardware store, a lady was cleaning a very dirty floor with a very sad mop. The mop looked up at the new mops hanging on the shelves and said "Someday, you will leave the shop and you will be a slave like me. You will be dipped in a bucket of water and made to mop dirty floors.

You will be dipped over and over again in dirty water squeezed until all the water drains from you and swished back and forth across the floor.

One of the mops hanging on the shelves said "We are floor cleaning slaves. We clean the floors of shops, houses, buildings and toilets. We will become smelly and dirty then thrown away like rubbish. That is what our life is. The humans squeeze the life out of us. One day soon someone will buy you and use you as a slave. "

None of the new mops on the shelves like to hear that. Now we dreaded being bought by anyone.

Then one day an old lady came to the hardware store to buy a mop. In a panic I said "Please don't pick me! Please don't pick me!" But after looking at all of the mops, she did pick me. She rubbed my hair over and over again, smiling. "You have to go to work," just like the old mop told us" said the other new mops hanging on the shelf. I cried "Goodbye," and went away with the old lady.

The old lady took me home and put me in her sewing room where there only carpet that I couldn't clean.

I sat there for a few days, wondering when I would be put to work. Then the old lady came to the sewing room and took off my handle. Then she made a head, hands, and a body. She made me into a beautiful doll! She smiled at me and said "I will name you Mopparella, and you will be May's best friend." May, her granddaughter came to live with her after her mum and dad were killed in a car accident. She looked after May all alone and needed a helper and friend for May.

Then she chanted a magic spell over me.

"Mop doll! Mop doll!
With Molly's eyes!
And Polly's voice!
Come alive! Come alive!
Carmen's Power!
I'll give you skills to
Talk and dance
To tell a story
To sing a song
And to keep my darling granddaughter May sound asleep."

"I am a live doll! I am a live doll!" said Mopparella.

I became alive. Now I knew I was not going to be a slave like the other mops. She made me nice lace dresses and a hat and said to me "You are not going to be a cleaning lady; you will be my granddaughter's doll. You will live in my granddaughter May's closet and tell her bed time stories until she goes to sleep. You will be given all the skills needed to be an entertainer. Your name is Mopparella and you will sing and dance and tell stories to my granddaughter May." Then she taught me a mop dance.

"Hop! Hop! Dolly mop!

Swirl and Sweep

Jump and leap

Sing and dance

for my darling little May."

"You will only come out at night," said the old lady. I came out every night and sang and danced and told bedtime stories. May sometimes cuddled me and took me to bed with her.

In the morning I was put back inside the closet. My bed time stories were very entertaining and the little girl May went to sleep without any problems. The old lady looked after me and her granddaughter.

—

She made me many new clothes and gave me many new skills. Then one day a new little girl came to play with her granddaughter May. The more stories I told the more power I gained and I went to other little girls' houses and told them bedtime stories. The old lady did not know that I went out of her house to tell stories to other children. I visited many children and told them many bedtime stories and made many children go to sleep. Whenever children were having a hard time sleeping they called for Mopparella.

While I was out entertaining another little girl, May woke up and cried and her grandma looked for me to put May back to sleep. I wasn't in the closet and I wasn't on the bed with May. To grandma's amazement I came through the window like a flying angel.

Grandma didn't know that I had gained the power to fly outside of her house. Grandma asked me where I had been, so I told her about the little girl I went to see. Her named is Jacqueline and she is the daughter of Byran the King of the underworld. The little child sleeps with the old and the sick and she has no one to tell her bedtime stories. She sleeps in her rags with her old teddy bear wrapped in a paper.

She told me that once she lived in a house with beautiful things and had a special chair set aside for her and she was called "Princess Jacquline." One day some murderous and thieves rampaged through her house. Her family died trying to fight the thieves. Jacquline hid under her bed and when the thieves were gone, she left her home and walked through the streets into the forest. She didn't have a cape like Little Red Riding Hood to keep her warm and safe from the wolves.

She wasn't kissed by a frog to turn her back into a beautiful princess. She had to sleep with the snakes and bugs and she didn't have a cup to drink water from the river. Then a wild bushman led her to a stream where sparking water shone like stars were floating over it. He showed the little girl Jacquline how to make a cup from a leaf and asked her to drink some of the sparkling water.

Her face lit up in the mirror of the water.

She had a tiara on her head and her teddy bear was new with bright eyes. To protect Jacquline from evil, the water from the stream turned her into an orphan with ragged dress and her jewels and fine clothes floated away in the stream.

Jacquline lived with street people and who protected her but they didn't know any bedtime stories. Now and then Jacquline went back to the stream to look at her reflection to remind her that she is still a princess.

I told her a story about a princess called Titi. Titi's father, King Toran lost the war and his kingdom. He didn't have a son to be trained as a Prince or a King, so his only daughter had to learn the skills.

The little princess had to take over the throne one day,

therefore she had to live with her people as one of them and had to learn all the life skills of the people and her kingdom. She had to become poor and no one in the kingdom knew she was a princess. She learned all about the King Damas who overthrew her father's kingdom.

She secretly recruited men and trained them to fight against King Damas. She became a warrior Princess. She had learned to fight with swords and arrows. She dressed like a King and no one knew she was a princess inside a king's costume. Her trained army trusted her. She was fighting for her people. King Damas wasn't a good king. He sent the people's tax money to his society and deprived King Toran's people. Everyone hated him. One day princess Titi and her trained army surrounded King Damas and the castle. He fought with all his army and lost to princess Titi and her soldiers. Princess Titi took her helmet off her head in triumphant and showed her face. All the kingdom's people shouted "Princess Titi! Princess Titi!" She was crowned as Queen and took over the kingdom. Everyone was happy and cheered the Queen Titi.

The story of Princess Titi made Jacquline happy in her sleep and she dreamt about herself as a princess.

That was how she coped with her situation and when Jacquline grows up she will return to the stream, gather her belongings and she live as a princess. Grandma was pleased that Mopparella was helping other children. While they were talking about the lost princess, May fell asleep again.

Mopparella helped many children go to sleep and dream about magical things.

Then Mopparella heard the call of another girl and went to her. She was from Russia and her name was Mashusky. She had lost all of her family in the Chernobyl nuclear accident. She was adopted by two strange people from a far away place. Mashusky enjoyed her life with them. When she was seven she was diagnosed with cancer. All her hair fell out and she began wearing a red scarf in memory of Russia. She sat on the hospital bed all alone and she didn't know anyone except her adopted parents. They visited her often, but she didn't have anyone to read her bedtime stories at night so she could sleep well. She feared she may die soon, in a strange land. She missed Russia very much. Her memories of Russia were very precious to her. Mopparella came and talked to Mashusky about the life of an angel. Mopparella told her that if you die at a young age and didn't get to live very long in this world, you will go to heaven and become an angel. This made Mashusky happy. Mashusky's face lit up like an angel. Mopparella told her "You will have wings and the power to have anything you want. You can have any toy you want. There is no sickness or unhappiness in heaven. In the angel world you live three centuries and go through six pairs of wings. Just imagine Mashusky you will be able to fly over beautiful flowers and in the blue sky. You'll meet new angel friends and you won't be alone."

Mopparella's magical skills took Mashusky into the magical world of angels. They were singing and dancing and playing with all sorts of toys. Mashusky learnt to fly in the magical world of angels. Moparella gave her the hope of a new world where she would be free. Mopparella said "Whenever you are sad, Mashusky, think of the heavenly place and enjoy a magical dream."

She told her a story about a woman called Dina who tried to change the world so accidents like the Chernobyl nuclear accident would not happen.

Dina was very unhappy with the world. She was mad about everything. She complained about everything and was very upset. Dina wanted the world to be in peace. She wanted the world to be beautiful. She wanted the birds and animals to be free and happy and live in the forests. Dina didn't want the forests to be destroyed.

She was very angry about people killing animals and wearing furs.

She didn't even want to eat meat and she became a vegetarian. "A perfect world what I want," she sighed. She wrote books against forest destructions, she marched against killing whales. She was very unhappy with the world. Dina told everyone that they are doing the wrong thing.

She was the maddest woman you have ever seen, until one day she visited an art gallery. It was peaceful and quiet in the gallery. She looked at many paintings about the present, past and future. All the paintings made sense to her.

She went to the shop and bought canvas, paint and brushes. She painted the forests before they were destroyed. She painted the town before it was modernised. She painted the animals before they were domesticated. She created a world of peace in her art works. Her world was pretty and peaceful. She found peace in her imagination.

Dina was totally consumed by her paintings and she wasn't mad anymore but she still communicated with the wrong doers through her art.

After the story Mashusky fell asleep and Mopparella flew away.

Mopparella went to a home with thirteen children. The youngest of the thirteen children was Salina. Because there were lots of children in the house, her mum and dad were very busy. They didn't have time to read her bedtime stories. They had to get up very early to send all the children to school, and because of that they all had to go to bed early. Salina couldn't sleep and was yearning for someone to read her bedtime stories.

Mopparella came and sat next to her. First Mopparella listened to Salina tell her that she never had any new clothes, they were all hand-me-downs and because she was the youngest in the family she only got hand-me-downs as Christmas presents as well. Salina was very sad. Her dreams were not filled with magic. It was so hard for her parents to buy presents for them all.

Then Mopparella told her a story about a little girl called Penny. Penny did not have anyone to tell her bed time stories. Her mum and dad were very busy and ignored Penny. Her brother and sisters could read to her but they were busy too. She was desperate to read so she opened up a book. Penny didn't understand the words and only the pictures made her happy.

When she saw a picture of a horse, Penny made up her own story that she rode the horse. The horse took her into a dark forest where monsters were having a party. She was scared and didn't like it there. Then the horse took her to a beautiful garden of fairies. The fairies dressed in fairy clothes and played with her. She was happy in a beautiful place.

Then Penny saw a picture of a fish in a book she made up a story that she turned into a mermaid and swam underwater. She found treasures from an old ship. She became a rich girl and lived a happy life.

Penny made up many stories and looked at the pictures and words in the books. Slowly she connected the pictures to the words and learnt to read. One day Penny realised she could read. From then on she read many new stories to herself. She taught herself many new skills and made herself many new things. When she wasn't capable of doing something she used her imagination to make herself happy. Mopparella told her many stories and lead her into the magical world of imagination. Salina went to sleep with a smile.

Whenever Salina wanted to sleep she went into the magical world of imagination that Mopparella showed her.

Salina was happy because her imaginations lead her to wild and wonderful places.

Mopparella met a boy at an orphanage. His name was Martin. He was moved from orphanage to orphanage. He was very sad and no one ever visited him. He never had any Christmas presents. His nights were lonely and he had trouble sleeping.

Mopparella saw his sadness and he couldn't imagine anything happy or magical.

Mopparella gave him a magical doll that he could tell all his troubles to. She transformed this sad boy and led him into the magical world of imagination. Mopparella told him that whenever he was sad or needed anything, all he had to do was close his eyes and enter the magical world of imagination, where he could talk and play with anyone and anything. Mopparella told him a story about an orphan called Stephen who was very lonely. He didn't have anything fun to do. Every day boring chores kept him sad and busy. One day he sat outside the orphanage garden and watched some ants.

Each ant took a piece of a dead caterpillar and put it in the ants' nest. It was a struggle for the ants to carry all the pieces of the caterpillar, but they work together and did it.

Stephen found a hole in the ground, surrounded by stones. He was bored, so he picked up the stones one by one and threw them into the hole. Some fell in the hole some didn't. It was fun trying to throw the stones in the hole.

Some other boys walked past and watched what Stephen was doing. Stephen asked the boys to join in the game of throwing stones in the hole, and they did. Then they gave themselves points for each stone landed in the hole. The person with the most stones in the hole got most points and he was the winner.

It was fun and everyone enjoyed the game. Stephen had invented the game of stones that is now played with marbles.

The orphan boys became friends and played the game often. A bond started to build between them. They were happy and made the most of their situation. With Mopparella's magical bedtime stories Martin's sadness slowly disappeared and he learnt to imagine happy and magical things. Martin turned into a happy child through listening to Mopparella's magical bedtime stories.

Mopparella visited a rich girl who had all the toys, clothes and jewellery a girl could want. She could had anything she wanted. Her name was Susie Anne and she lived at a boarding school most of the time. When she came home on school holidays her mum and dad were very busy and she had no one to read her bedtime stories.

Susie Anne wanted to be with her parents and most of the time she was very lonely. Her dreams were so sad and scary. Mopparella told her a story about a very rich King. His castle was full of gold; his throne was made of emeralds and diamonds. People showered the King with gold, silver and gems. Everywhere he looked there were gold, silver, gems, valuable paintings and ornaments. Wealth! Wealth! That was all surrounded him.

Everyone admired the King and said "King is rich so he must be happy."

The King wasn't happy.

The King wasn't happy until one day he sat in the garden on a garden bench. He looked at the flowers, birds and the bees. Then a bird flew in and sat next to him on the garden bench. He fed the bird with some seeds. The bird wasn't scared it chirped.

The King was happy to have a pet. It sat on the Kings hand and ate the seeds. The bird came everyday and ate seeds from his hands. That little bird made the King happier than all the wealth in the world. He didn't have to be a King with the bird. And with the bird he was a free man.

Mopparella told her many magical bedtime stories that brought happiness and put a smile on many children. Through the bedtime stories Mopparella lead Susie Anne into the magical world of imagination. Susie Anne enjoyed her time with Mopparella and the magical world. Susie Anne caught falling stars and rode on a silvery moon and flew on white clouds. In her magical world of imagination, angels and fairies made the bedtime stories come alive. Susie Anne's dreams started to become happy and magical. Most nights she slept well. Mopparella helped her smile and enjoy the magical world of imagination.

Mopparella regularly visited many children. Her magical world of imagination took sad children into the world of happiness. They dreamt about the sky, the moon, clouds and all sorts of magical places where a child could be free and happy. Mopparella's shining wings shone on every child she visited.

Every night children were looking forward to listening to Mopparella's bedtime stories. Mopparella made everyone smile and enjoy a peaceful night of sleep.

The End